Published by
Louis Weber, C.E.O.
Publications International, Ltd.
7373 North Cicero Avenue
Lincolnwood, Illinois 60712

Ground Floor, 59 Gloucester Place
London W1U 8JJ

www.pilbooks.com

ISBN 1-4127-3712-5

The alarm is sounding at the Tonka Fire Station! All the firefighters stop what they're doing and hurry to help out. Help the firefighters by finding these things they'll need before leaving the station.

A hand-held radio

A hydrant wrench

A bullhorn

Fireman Fred

A nozzle

A map

Fire Chief Williams

Spark the Firedog

Officer O'Malley and the other rookie police officers are completing their training on the driving courses. When they're finished, no getaway cars will be able to get away from them! Find O'Malley and the things he'll need to pass his tests today.

Officer O'Malley

This motorcycle helmet

Keys

Handcuffs

A police dispatch radio

A utility belt

A notepad and pencil

A spare tire

The heavy work of expanding Hilldale Hospital requires heavy equipment! As the construction crews complete their work, you need to work on finding everything below.

Foreman Smith

Hammer

Drill

Pail

Safety glasses

Tape measure

Blueprints

Tool belt

Today's the day for the big Air and Water Show, and everyone's out in style! Everything that can fly or float is showing off a bit today. Show off your finding skills by picking out some of our friends at the show.

Otto-Pilot the Robot

Peg the Sea Dog

Pilot Jane

Gary the Glider

Co-pilot Carl

Hovercraft Harry

Captain Jack

The machines have as much fun as anyone at the State Fair! From the Monster Truck Rally to the Tractor Pull, everyone has a good time. Enjoy yourself while helping Farmer Howard find a new tractor so he won't have to use his old tools anymore.

Farmer Howard

Milking stool and pail

Scythe

Plow

Hoe

Scarecrow

A new tractor

Pitchfork

This town is already buried in snow, and the white stuff just keeps falling! Luckily, the heavy snow removal equipment is on the job. Lacey would like to help, but she's too young to drive, and she's misplaced her snow shovel and clothes! Can you help her out?

Mittens

Snow Shovel

Earmuffs

Lacey

Hat

Snowsuit

Boots

Scarf

It's late at night, and Mack's working overtime on a recycling truck. He's got to fix the hydraulic lifters so the truck will work in the morning! Help Mack find all the tools he needs to get the job done on time.

A hydraulic valve

A can of hydraulic fluid

A screwdriver

A grease gun

A torque wrench

A manual

A crowbar

The dam has broken and the flood waters are rising! But the rescue helicopters, boats, and vehicles are rescuing folks as fast as they can. As fast as you can, search for and rescue these "R" things:

Really sleepy bear

Raccoon

Ranger Roger

Rabbit

Rock climber

Rainbow trout

Red-tailed hawk

Rod and reel

RANGER STATION

FOREST RESCUE

Tonka

STATION #1

In all the hurry and excitement of leaving the firehouse, some firemen left behind some important items. Can you find their forgotten gear?

- ☐ Rope
- ☐ Fireman Fred's badge
- ☐ Spark the Firedog's collar
- ☐ Fire Chief Williams's lucky yellow suspenders
- ☐ Watch
- ☐ Flashlight

All the policemen are practicing driving. Practice your detective skills by going back and finding these items.

- ☐ Binoculars
- ☐ Walkie talkie
- ☐ Box of donuts
- ☐ Book of mug shots
- ☐ Wanted poster for Boris Badguy
- ☐ Policeman's Ball tickets

Go back to the hospital construction site and use your keen sight to pick out all these things.

- ☐ Toolbox
- ☐ Wheelbarrow
- ☐ Hand saw
- ☐ A lost work glove
- ☐ Bubble-gum bubble
- ☐ Spilled cup of coffee

Oops! Everyone lost something in the crowds at the Air and Water Show. Return these things to their rightful owners.

- ☐ Pilot Jane's flight notebook
- ☐ Co-pilot Carl's sunglasses
- ☐ Otto-Pilot the Robot's oilcan
- ☐ Gary the Glider's propeller
- ☐ Harry the Hovercraft's anchor
- ☐ Captain Jack's life preserver
- ☐ Peg the Sea Dog's bone